Baby Kermit's
Playtime
ABC

By Lily Jones
Illustrated by David Prebenna

A MUPPET PRESS/GOLDEN PRESS BOOK

AIRPLANES FLYING ROUND AND ROUND,

BLOCKS FOR **BUILDING** ON THE GROUND.

COLOR CRAYONS,

C

DOLLS TO **DRESS,**

ERASERS TO **ERASE** A MESS.

FINGER-PAINTING ON THE **FLOOR.**

GAMES ARE FUN. LET'S PLAY SOME MORE!

HIDE-AND-SEEK . . .

I HID IN HERE!

I

JACKS AND **JUMP** ROPES NOW APPEAR.

KERMIT'S KITE FLIES HIGH ABOVE.

LOTS OF **LITTLE** BOOKS TO **LOVE.**

MARBLES ROLLING ON THE FLOOR.

NO NOISE AT **NAPTIME!**
CLOSE THE DOOR.

ORANGE ORANGES TO EAT.

PIANO PRACTICE IS A TREAT.

A **QUILT** FOR DOLLY,

Q

ROCKING HORSE,

R

SWINGING MEANS A PUSH, OF COURSE!

TRAIN CARS MOVING IN A LINE,

UMBRELLAS AND . . .

A VALENTINE.

WAGON WHEELS HEAD WHO-KNOWS-WHERE,

XYLOPHONE MUSIC FILLS THE AIR.

YO-YOS SPINNING, RED AND BLUE,

AND **ZEBRAS** IN MY LITTLE **ZOO**!